Teggs is no ordinary dinosaur –
he's an **ASTROSAUR!** Captain of
the amazing spaceship DSS *Sauropod*,
he goes on dangerous missions and
fights evil – along with his faithful
crew, Gipsy, Arx and Iggy.

For more astro-fun visit the website
www.astrosaurs.co.uk

D0334554

Read all the adventures of
Teggs, Gipsy, Arx and Iggy!

RIDDLE OF THE RAPTORS
THE HATCHING HORROR
THE SEAS OF DOOM
THE MIND-SWAP MENACE
THE SKIES OF FEAR
THE SPACE GHOSTS
DAY OF THE DINO-DROIDS
THE TERROR-BIRD TRAP
THE PLANET OF PERIL
THE STAR PIRATES
THE CLAWS OF CHRISTMAS
THE SUN-SNATCHERS
REVENGE OF THE FANG
THE CARNIVORE CURSE
THE DREAMS OF DREAD
THE ROBOT RAIDERS
THE TWIST OF TIME
THE SABRE-TOOTH SECRET
THE FOREST OF EVIL
EARTH ATTACK!
THE T-REX INVASION

Read the full set of Astrosaurs Academy adventures!

DESTINATION: DANGER!
CONTEST CARNAGE!
TERROR UNDERGROUND!
JUNGLE HORROR!
DEADLY DRAMA!
CHRISTMAS CRISIS!
VOLCANO INVADERS!
SPACE KIDNAP!

Find out more at www.astrosaurs.co.uk

Astrosaurs

THE CASTLE OF FRANKENSAUR

Steve Cole

Illustrated by Woody Fox

RED FOX

THE CASTLE OF FRANKENSAUR
A RED FOX BOOK 978 1 849 41404 3

First published in Great Britain by Red Fox,
an imprint of Random House Children's Publishers UK
A Random House Group Company

First Red Fox edition published 2012

1 3 5 7 9 10 8 6 4 2

Text copyright © Steve Cole, 2012
Cover illustration and cards © Dynamo Design, 2012
Map © Charlie Fowkes, 2005
Illustrations by Woody Fox © Random House Children's Publishers UK, 2012

The Random House Group Limited supports the Forest Stewardship Council
(FSC®), the leading international forest certification organization. Our
books carrying the FSC label are printed on FSC®-certified paper. FSC is
the only forest certification scheme endorsed by the leading environmental
organizations, including Greenpeace. Our paper procurement policy can be
found at www. www.randomhouse.co.uk/environment.

Typeset in Bembo MT Schoolbook 16/20pt
by Falcon Oast Graphic Art Ltd.

Red Fox Books are published by Random House Children's Publishers UK,
61–63 Uxbridge Road, London W5 5SA

www.**randomhousechildrens**.co.uk
www.**randomhouse**.co.uk

Addresses for companies within The Random House Group Limited can
be found at: www.randomhouse.co.uk/offices.htm

THE RANDOM HOUSE GROUP Limited Reg. No. 954009

A CIP catalogue record for this book is available from the British Library.

Printed and bound in Great Britain by CPI Group (UK) Ltd,
Croydon, CR0 4YY

For Candi Scarlett Featherquill
(and Poppy Bristow, her inventive owner)

WARNING!

THINK YOU KNOW ABOUT DINOSAURS?

THINK AGAIN!

The dinosaurs . . .

Big, stupid, lumbering reptiles. Right?

All they did was eat, sleep and roar a bit. Right?

Died out millions of years ago when a big meteor struck the Earth. Right?

Wrong!

The dinosaurs weren't stupid. They may have had small brains, but they used them well. They had big thoughts and big dreams.

By the time the meteor hit, the last dinosaurs had already left Earth for ever. Some breeds had discovered how to travel through space as early as the Triassic period, and were already enjoying a new life among the stars. No one has found evidence of dinosaur technology yet. But the first fossil bones were only unearthed in 1822, and new finds are being made all the time.

The proof is out there, buried in the ground.

And the dinosaurs live on, way out in space, even now. They've settled down in a place they call the Jurassic Quadrant and over the last sixty-five million years they've gone on evolving.

The dinosaurs we'll be meeting are

 part of a special group called the Dinosaur Space Service. Their job is to explore space, to go on exciting missions and to fight evil and protect the innocent!

These heroic herbivores are not just dinosaurs.

They are *astrosaurs*!

NOTE: The following story has been translated from secret Dinosaur Space Service records. Earthling dinosaur names are used throughout, although some changes have been made for easy reading. There's even a guide to help you pronounce the dinosaur names on the next page.

Talking Dinosaur!

How to say the prehistoric
names in this book . . .

STEGOSAURUS -
STEG-oh-SORE-us

HADROSAUR -
HAD-roh-sore

DIMORPHODON -
die-MORF-oh-don

KRITOSAURUS -
CRY-tuh-SORE-us

DASPLETOSAURUS -
Dass-PLEE-tu-SORE-us

TRICERATOPS -
try-SERRA-tops

SAUROPELTA -
SORE-uh-PELT-ah

THE CREW OF THE
DSS SAUROPOD

**CAPTAIN
TEGGS STEGOSAUR**

ARX ORANO,
FIRST OFFICER

GIPSY SAURINE,
COMMUNICATIONS
OFFICER

IGGY TOOTH,
CHIEF ENGINEER

Jurassic Quadrant

Ankylos

Steggos

Noxia-

Diplox

INDEPENDENT
DINOSAUR
ALLIANCE

vegetarian
sector

Squawk
Major

DSS
UNION OF
PLANETS

PTEROSAURIA

Tri System

Corytho

Lambeos

Aqua Minor

Iguanos

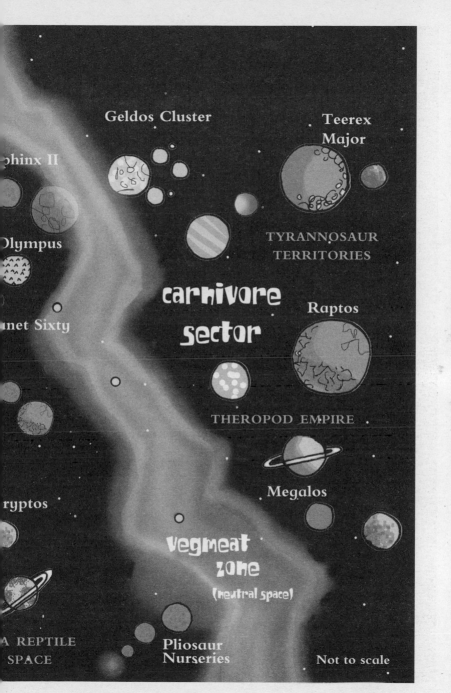

THE CASTLE OF FRANKENSAUR

Chapter One

ROBBERY IN SPACE

"Help! This is Pilot Marsh in star-vault Zeta Three *– I am under attack!"*

Captain Teggs Stegosaur almost jumped out of his orange–brown skin as the urgent voice echoed around his spaceship, the DSS *Sauropod*.

"A distress call!" he cried. "Luckily I've got the best ship in space and the finest crew in the universe. Astrosaurs to the rescue!"

Teggs galloped over to Gipsy Saurine, the stripy hadrosaur in charge of communications. "Gipsy, can you trace where Pilot Marsh's message came from?"

"On the case, Captain." Gipsy peered at her computer screen. "It came from two star-systems away. And it was sent on a 'priority red' channel."

"*Emergency*," came the pilot's voice again. "*Star-vault Zeta Three is under attack from an unidentified spacecraft. My location is Sector Three-point-seven-nine . . .*"

"What is a star-vault, anyway?" asked Teggs.

"It's like a giant safe that's been turned into a spaceship, Captain," called a green triceratops from across the flight deck. This was Arx, Teggs's brainy first

officer. "They are used by galactic banks
to transport gold and jewels between
planets in the Vegetarian Sector. No ship
in space is tougher to get into."

"Even so, it sounds like a tasty target
for robbers." At the word "tasty"
Teggs's tum rumbled – no matter what
the emergency, Teggs never lost his
enormous appetite! "Set a course to
intercept that star-vault. Maximum
speed!"

At the captain's command, his flight crew of miniature flying reptiles – fifty formidable dimorphodon – flapped into action, working the ship's controls with beaks and claws. With a mighty rush of engines, the *Sauropod* zoomed away.

"*I need help!*" Yet again, Pilot Marsh's voice boomed from the speakers. "*Hostile creatures have destroyed the ship's weapons and broken in.*"

Arx looked flabbergasted. "I can't believe that anything could get inside a star-vault so quickly!"

Gipsy switched on her communicator. "Pilot Marsh, this is the DSS *Sauropod*. We're on our way."

"Can you identify your attackers?" Teggs asked the pilot.

"*Two meat-eating dinosaurs in spacesuits . . . they're coming towards me now . . .*" Pilot Marsh sounded terrified. "*No . . . it's not two dinosaurs . . . By all the moons of Mobbalop, it's a monster! A horrible, terrible MONSTER! Keep back! Don't—!*"

Suddenly the voice was cut off.

Arx looked grave. Gipsy's head-crest flushed blue with alarm. The dimorphodon shivered and shook their beaks.

"That poor pilot," Teggs muttered. "How long till we reach him?"

"Ten minutes," said Arx.

"Too slow." Teggs reared up. "Gipsy, get Iggy on the scanner. Quickly!"

Gipsy tapped some controls, and a few seconds later the image of a tough iguanodon in a cap appeared on the big screen before them. Iggy was the *Sauropod*'s chief engineer, so it was hardly surprising that he was reporting from the engine room.

"Iggy, we have a star-vault in big trouble," said Teggs, "and maximum speed just isn't fast enough."

"Then it's a good job the canteen served an extra-hot fig curry last night." Iggy turned to the engineers behind him. "Lads, we need a five-star fuel injection. Fetch this morning's whiffiest dung buckets, on the double!"

Teggs smiled grimly. Dinosaur spaceships were powered by burning dung – the nastier the poo, the faster you flew!

Within thirty seconds, Iggy and his workforce had emptied their toxic buckets into the dung-burners – and the *Sauropod*

shot forward so fast that
Teggs was thrown to
the floor.

"That's
better!"
Gipsy yelled over
the roar of the
engines, clinging to
her controls. "Now we
should reach *Zeta Three* in
under two minutes."

"But something else will
reach us first!" Arx called in
warning. "Space radar shows a small
object on a collision course . . ."

"Put it on the scanner," said Teggs.
"Magnify the image."

"Eep!" Sprite, the dimorphodon leader, rushed to obey.

Iggy's image faded, to be replaced by the dark infinity of space. A small point of light was hurtling towards the astrosaurs.

"It's a missile!" squealed Gipsy, and the dimorphodon began to cheep and chitter.

"No . . . wait." Teggs was studying the screen intently. "I think . . . it's an escape pod."

"A lifeboat in space?" Arx checked his controls and nodded. "You're right, Captain. It must have ejected from the *Zeta Three*."

"Sauropod, *this is Pilot Marsh*." The voice was fainter this time, so Gipsy quickly pumped up the volume. "*I've been kicked off my star-vault. I tried to tell them*

8

I wasn't carrying any money, but they didn't care. They said they'd zap me with lasers if I didn't leave in this escape pod . . ."

"You're safe now, Marsh," said Teggs. "We will use space-magnets to pull you to us. Don't worry, we'll catch these crooks."

"Eeep!" said Sprite, flapping over to the magnet controls.

"One minute till we reach *Zeta Three*, Captain," warned Gipsy.

"Wait . . . it's changing course." Arx flicked some switches on the space radar. "Now it's heading towards Sector Four."

Gipsy looked puzzled. "But there's nothing out there apart from a few asteroids."

"Nothing that *we* know of," Teggs corrected her. "Arx, the moment we're

9

in range, fire dung-torpedoes *and* lasers.
That should slow down those robbers."

"They seem to be slowing down
already," Arx reported. "What are they
up to?"

Teggs watched as the star-vault came
into view on the scanner screen. It was a
huge steel cylinder, covered in gigantic
chains and padlocks. Suddenly it turned
sharply towards a large asteroid.

"They must be trying to take
cover behind that space rock," said Teggs.
"Sprite, steer us between them and the
asteroid. Arx – OPEN FIRE!"

Arx jabbed a button with his nose-horn and sent twin torpedoes trailing away into space. *Fa-TOOM! Ba-TOOOM!* Smelly brown explosions shook the star-vault. At the same time, the triceratops tugged on a lever that fired blisteringly bright laser beams. *Zeta Three* smoked and shook.

"We've burst its fuel tanks!" Arx beamed. "It can't get far now!"

Teggs crossed quickly to the communicator. "Attention," he said sternly. "This is the DSS *Sauropod*. You have attacked and stolen a plant-eater

11

star-vault. Surrender at once."

"Captain, look!" Gipsy pointed past him. "They're transmitting to our scanner."

Teggs turned to find a smoking control room coming into focus on the big screen – and gasped as a monstrous figure was revealed.

At first he took it to be a meat-eating dinosaur in a spacesuit, with a fierce green head and jaws crammed with teeth. There was another carnivore behind it, with blood-red skin and fangs that were just as forbidding. Then, with a shock, he saw that the red neck was attached to the green body . . .

"I don't believe it," he breathed. "That dinosaur has got two heads!"

"You ask us to surrender?" hissed the green head. "Never! Soon we shall destroy your kind for ever!"

Chapter Two

THE ASTEROID

For a few moments Teggs was lost for words. He saw that as well as two heads, the creature had two different-sized tails, one with an arm growing out of it. Three more arms sprouted from its chest, and while it stood on two green legs, a red pair poked out of the creature's butt. It looked as if two different dinosaurs had been squashed together.

"Your threats don't scare us," Teggs told the double-headed monster. "It's *you* who should be afraid. You've committed a very serious crime – hijack!"

"Oh, hello," the monster's red head replied. "How did you know my name was Jack?"

"Shut up!"
the green
head growled
at the red one.
"He wasn't
saying *Hi,
Jack*, he was
saying *hijack*."

"Hello," said
Jack's red head again.

"I said, SHUT UP!" the green head
roared.

Gipsy looked baffled. "I've heard of the
saying, *Two heads are better than one*, but . . ."

"Not in this case," said Arx.

"It seems our hijacker has a split
personality," Teggs murmured. "All
right, Hijacker Jack whoever-you-are.
You destroyed that star-vault's weapons
as you came aboard, and we've just
blown open your fuel tanks. You *have* to
surrender – it's your only choice."

15

"Wrong," the green head hissed through his greasy lips. "We have one weapon left."

Suddenly the scanner screen went dark.

"He's cut the signal," Gipsy reported, "and started up the engines."

Teggs frowned. "He can't escape without fuel."

"He's not running away." Arx jumped back from his instruments. "*Zeta Three*'s heading straight for the *Sauropod* – at a thousand miles per hour!"

Teggsgroaned. "Of course, his last weapon – the star-vault itself, tough enough to smash us out of space!" He leaped into

his control pit.
"Gipsy – shields
on! Sprite, get us
out of here – full
throttle – *GO!*"

The dimorphodon
squealed and pecked at
the controls, and with
a sudden surge of supercharged
engines, the *Sauropod* veered aside. Teggs
clung on, teeth clenched, eyes shut.
Until . . .

"It missed us by millimetres!" Arx
whooped.

Gipsy clutched her tummy as the
dimorphodon flapped down beside her,
panting for breath. "Phew! That was *way*
too close."

"The asteroid behind us will be too
close for *Zeta Three* to avoid," said Teggs,
eating a small branch while he got his
breath back. "The ship will crash-land
for sure. Put it on the scanner, Gipsy."

Gipsy obeyed, and the astrosaurs watched as the chunky star-vault whooshed towards the giant rock. Within seconds it was lost from sight – and soon after, a cloud of white smoke rose from the asteroid's barren surface.

"It's landed hard," Arx said, scanning his instruments. "Hijacker Jack may not have survived."

"I hope he has," said Gipsy. "We need to find out more about him, and where he came from. Shall I send a recording of Jack to DSS HQ? They can check their criminal data-files for two-headed dino-monsters."

"Good idea." Teggs sighed worriedly. "*Soon we shall destroy your kind for ever*, he said."

"I'd like to find his friends in the spaceship that attacked *Zeta Three*," said Arx. "How did they beat its defences so fast?"

"There's a major mystery brewing

here, I'm sure of it," said Teggs. "Once Pilot Marsh is aboard, we'll all go down with Iggy to check the wreck — and get some answers . . ."

It didn't take long for the *Sauropod* to drag the little space lifeboat on board. Teggs welcomed Pilot Marsh with a big mug of swamp tea.

"Thanks for saving me, Captain." Marsh was a gruff sauropelta with tattoos of plants on his arms and legs, and a red spotted hankie tied round his head. "By the five moons of Queebly, I'm glad you didn't let that two-headed piece of space-trash get away."

Teggs steered him along a corridor towards the shuttle bay. "We're going to see what's left of *Zeta Three* right now. Was there really nothing of value on board?"

"Not a bean. I'd just delivered some gold to Steggos, and was on my way to pick up some jewels from Olympus." Marsh shook his head. "A small spaceship came out of nowhere. First my weapons stopped working . . . then, somehow, that thing punched a big hole in the star-vault's side – through six metres of solid steel!"

As Teggs and Marsh reached the bay, thick smoke was pouring from the exhaust of the speediest craft, Shuttle Alpha – Iggy had already started up the engines.

Arx and Gipsy saluted through the open door. "We're ready to go, Captain!"

Teggs introduced Pilot Marsh to his crew. Within seconds, the astrosaurs and

their guest were sealed inside, and Shuttle
Alpha rocketed away into the blackness
of space.

The asteroid was soon filling their
view through the windscreen – a barren,
bumpy rock.

"It's only sixty miles across," said Iggy.
"We'll fly low overhead till we spot the
wreck. Shouldn't take us long . . ."

Gipsy pointed out a huddle of strange
lumpy markings on the rocky surface.

"Hey, what are they?"

"Bless my horns, there are old buildings down there." Arx peered intently as the shapes grew clearer the closer they came. "It must have been a village, long ago."

"And look, Marsh!" said Teggs, spying the gleam of starlight on steel down below. "There's *Zeta Three*."

"Strike me green and call me Horace." Marsh scratched his hankie-covered head. "You're right!"

"Well spotted, Captain." Iggy hit the jet-brakes as the shuttle passed over the buckled, broken star-vault on the ground below. "It's crashed a few miles away from that village."

Gipsy pointed through the windscreen again. "And about half a mile from that old castle!"

Teggs felt a prickle of foreboding at the sight of the spooky stronghold. The castle could've come straight out of a horror film. Big and dark, overgrown with ivy, it stood in the middle of a wild garden, leaning drunkenly to one side. Its tall towers were topped with crooked spires, like a giant clawed hand.

And at two of the upstairs windows, lights were blazing . . .

"So," Teggs murmured. "Someone lives on this old asteroid."

"Why ever would they want to?" wondered Gipsy.

"It's a good place to get up to stuff in secret," Arx suggested.

"Exactly," said Teggs. "Put us down by *Zeta Three*, Ig. We'll explore the wreck, then call on the castle. But we'd better change into our space armour first." A spark of excitement tickled his tail at the thought of the adventure ahead. "I don't know what we'll find out there – but I've got a feeling it's going to be dangerous!"

Chapter Three

THE WRECK AND THE CASTLE

Three minutes after touching down on the asteroid, the astrosaurs were good to go in battle mode.

Teggs wore his helmet and electro-tail armour that could zap any enemies. Gipsy, the queen of unarmed combat, had changed into her tough blue dino-judo suit. Iggy was armed with a tail-guard and heavy-duty stun claws while Arx wore a special steel headdress with built-in horn blasters.

"You'd better dress for danger too, Pilot Marsh," said Teggs. "You'll find a spare helmet and some back armour in the store behind you."

"Thanks," said Marsh, squeezing into the shiny steel gear. "By Wongo's gut-wobbler . . . whatever's out there, we'll be ready for it."

"Let's hope so," said Gipsy softly, passing round torches.

As Iggy opened the shuttle doors, a freezing gale blew in. It was a wild night. The sky was black, but glowing meteors drifted slowly through the sky like strange clouds. The dinosaurs trooped down a rocky hillside towards the wreck of the star-vault, their torch-beams lighting the way.

Teggs and Arx wasted no time inspecting the gap in the side of the super-secure ship. And what they saw shocked them both.

"You said that Hijacker Jack broke in through steel that was six metres thick," Teggs reminded Marsh. "Well, he didn't."

"What do you mean?" The pilot shone his torch into the darkness.

"You can see the hole yourself."

"Yes," Arx agreed. "But the hole has been cut through solid *pumpkin*!"

Marsh hurried closer, Iggy and Gipsy just behind him. "Well, bake me a cake and call it Susan — you're right! This whole chunk of the spaceship's wall has turned into pumpkin!"

"And very delicious it is too," said Teggs, chomping on the edges of the orange hole.

"Now we know how Hijacker Jack got inside so fast," Gipsy observed. "It's easy to cut through a wall of pumpkin!"

"And look here!" Arx had moved further along the star-vault. "An enormous stick of celery poking out of the roof."

Marsh went very pale. "That . . . that used to be my laser cannon! How could it turn into a giant vegetable?"

"No idea." Iggy broke off some celery and showed it to Teggs. "I've never seen celery this size before."

"Well, *Zeta Three* wasn't like this when I took off," growled Marsh. "That hijacking wabber-worm and his friends must've done something to it while we were in flight."

Teggs nodded. "If we can find Hijacker Jack, perhaps we'll learn what."

The dinos climbed into the hole, and Pilot Marsh led the way through the star-vault's dark and crumpled corridors. The astrosaurs helped him search the whole ship, until finally they reached the control room.

And found it empty.

"Hey, look." Iggy pointed to the floor, which was covered in dust and broken glass from the crash – along with large dark marks. "Those look like footprints leading out of here."

"So Hijacker Jack *did* survive the crash," breathed Arx.

Marsh nodded. "But where in the name of Janky Poodle's six-legged space-dog is he now?"

"I think it's time we checked out
that old castle." Teggs led the way out
of the control room. "We saw lights
in the windows, so we know *someone's*
inside . . ."

It was starting to rain as the dinosaurs
left the shelter of the star-vault and
hurried back up the hillside. Teggs
shivered. The creepy castle loomed
ahead, its two lit windows like yellow
eyes watching him approach. The wind's
howl was like a ghostly warning.

Finally, with lightning forking through
the stormy skies above, the soaking
dinosaurs reached an enormous wild
garden that stretched around the castle.
Teggs led his friends along an overgrown
path and climbed the crooked steps to a
huge wooden front door.

Knocking loudly, Teggs turned to his
friends. "Get ready, everyone. We don't
know what we're going to meet in
here . . ."

SHUNK! THUNK! Heavy bolts were
drawn back on the other side of the door,
and a key rattled loudly in the lock.

Iggy raised his stun claws; Gipsy
adopted a judo pose; Arx got ready with

31

his horn blasters; and Teggs and Marsh raised their tails as the door creaked slowly open . . .

"DO NOT MOVE!" A big robot dinosaur appeared. It had a fierce face, red glowing eyes and a gleaming hunchback. Five steel ropes suddenly shot out from inside the steel hump.

"Hey!" Teggs gasped as the first rope wrapped around his arm and tightened. Arx, Iggy, Gipsy and Marsh were grabbed in the same split-second. As they cried out in shock, Teggs swung his spiky tail at the robot's head, but – *ZZZZT!* – a jolt of electricity zapped through his bones, knocking him to his knees.

"My name is IGOR – Intelligent 'Generation One' Robot," the thing told them in a flat, droning voice. "I can electrify these ropes. If you try to fight me, I shall do so."

"Charming!" said Gipsy, holding very still. "Do you treat all your visitors like this?"

"I obey Doctor Frankensaur's orders," IGOR replied.

"Frankensaur?" Arx looked shocked. "Doctor Vickavon Frankensaur?"

Marsh frowned. "You've heard of him?"

33

"Frankensaur was a genius," said Arx, nodding. "He worked for big electronics companies on Hadros Major, inventing new technology. But one day last year, right in the middle of a top-secret project, he went missing . . ."

"You know too much about my master," said IGOR. "Conclusion – you are spies, come to harm him."

"No!" Teggs cried. "That's not true—!"

"Electrifying ropes," the robot interrupted. "NOW!"

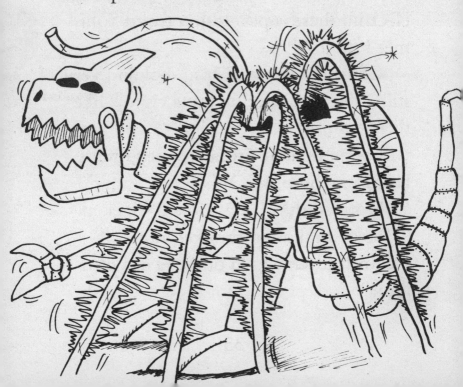

Chapter Four

WHAT'S THE MATTA?

ZZZZZT! Teggs gasped with pain as the steel cable around his arm sparked blue, sending powerful shocks through his whole body. His friends cried out as IGOR electrified the other ropes.

"Stop . . . it!" Teggs sank slowly to his knees. "We're not spies, we're ASTROSAURS!"

"Astrosaurs?" A large shadowy figure was approaching across the castle's hallway. "Stop, IGOR. Your master commands it!"

Obediently, the robot switched off the power. Arx, Iggy and Gipsy fell to the ground, panting for breath. Marsh groaned with relief.

Teggs looked up at the imposing dinosaur who'd given IGOR his orders. "So . . . you're Doctor Frankensaur?"

"That is correct," the figure replied. Frankensaur was a kritosaurus – similar in size and shape to Iggy but with a snout sticking out like a bony balloon. He wore a scarf and a long dark jacket, and seemed to have been in the wars – one of his arms was in plaster, supported by a large sling, while the end of his tail was swollen and wrapped in bandages. His words came slowly, as if he were half-asleep.

"And who exactly are you?"

Teggs pulled his red Captain's Card from his belt. "I am Teggs Stegosaur, and these are my crewmates, Arx, Gipsy and Iggy. You can trust us – my crew and I have top-level DSS security clearance."

"So I see." Frankensaur returned Teggs's card and turned to IGOR. "Release my guests at once. Get on with your duties."

The robot retracted his ropes, bowed and clanked away.

"Beats having a guard dog, I suppose," said Iggy.

"Indeed," said Frankensaur. "I built IGOR myself to keep me company – and to keep me safe." He turned slowly to Teggs. "Now, what are you doing here, Captain?"

"We're investigating the spaceship that crashed nearby," said Teggs.

"Oh. That." Frankensaur shook his head. "I was so busy working I didn't even notice until I glanced out of the window just now."

"You didn't notice a crashing star-vault?" Teggs raised his eyebrows. "Our friend Marsh here was the pilot – until a two-headed monster kicked him out. A two-headed monster who right now is on the loose, somewhere on this asteroid."

"I see." Frankensaur looked grave. "Please, come in."

Dripping water, Teggs and his friends followed Frankensaur into the cold, gloomy hall. A single electric bulb flickered above their heads. The walls were bare. A wooden staircase with floorboards

missing ran up into the darkness of the upper levels.

"What a dump!" Iggy murmured.

Frankensaur led his guests into a shabby sitting room, and invited them to sit on dusty couches. IGOR stood by a door on the far side.

"IGOR," said Frankensaur, "bring refreshments."

IGOR bowed and left the room.

"Do you actually live here, Doctor

Frankensaur?" Arx wondered. "A ramshackle old castle is the last place I'd expect to find a brilliant inventor like you."

"That is precisely why I stay." Frankensaur smiled coldly. "I had to leave Hadros Major to continue work on my special project. You see, a brilliant meat-eater scientist called Professor Hydra is trying to invent something similar. His agents very nearly succeeded in kidnapping me."

Arx nodded. "I suppose Hydra wanted your help."

"He needs my brain," Frankensaur agreed, staring into space.

"So you went into hiding," Teggs reasoned. "But why here?"

"This castle has been in my family for centuries," said Frankensaur. "It was

40

first built as a holiday home for a rich relative of mine. She even provided a little village nearby for all her servants." He sighed and stroked his bandaged tail. "I thought no one would ever find me here. Thought that I could carry on with my work in safety."

"What *is* this special project of yours?" asked Gipsy.

"You must tell us," Teggs said. "At first we thought the two-headed monster came here by accident. But perhaps he's come here to get you."

Frankensaur got to his feet. "I will show you. Come along . . ." He led the way out of the room and flicked a switch. Slowly, a bulb glowed into life in the cracked ceiling, lighting the rickety stairs.

"Doesn't look very safe." Iggy eyed Frankensaur's injuries – the bandaged lump on his tail and his arm in plaster. "Speaking of safety, what happened to you?"

"Pardon?" The doctor seemed lost in his own grim thoughts. "Oh, my injuries, you mean. I tripped and fell down this staircase in the dark – very careless of me. Luckily IGOR is programmed for first aid . . ."

The stairs led onto a shadowy landing lined with empty suits of cobwebby dino-armour, and stuffed plants mounted on the walls. Teggs and his friends followed the dino-doctor over to a large door.

"In here, you will find a masterpiece of technology." Frankensaur slowly opened the door and flicked another light-switch. "Behold!"

Teggs led the way eagerly inside, but he was confused by what he saw there.

"Er . . . it looks like two telescopes stuck to a big hairdryer that's pointing at an empty toilet cubicle."

"Looks can be deceiving," said Frankensaur with a smile. "You are in fact looking at my marvellous MATTA machine! MATTA – short for 'Mix-And-Transmit, Transmogrifying Area'."

Marsh looked blank. "What does transmogrify mean?"

"To change the form of something," Arx explained, "making it different."

"It works like this." Frankensaur walked stiffly over to the two "telescopes". "First, I choose the two things to be mixed and transmitted with these focus tubes. I shall point them at the garden below. Captain, choose any two vegetables."

"Certainly," said Teggs keenly. He looked through the tubes and spotted clumps of lettuces and ferns growing side by side. "I'll have one of each of those."

"I'm sure you like your veg on the large side." Frankensaur twisted a dial on the side of the machine. "Now, all I need to do is switch on the MATTA machine – and all *you* need to do is

44

watch that cubicle . . ."

Suddenly the hairdryer thing glowed bright green. A buzz of power filled the room – and then a large and curious shape began to form inside the vibrating cubicle.

It was part giant lettuce, part enormous fern . . .

"Amazing!" cried Arx, studying the MATTA machine as it powered down. "You transported two vegetables from the garden, combined them somehow, and made them reappear right here at six times their normal size!"

Teggs rushed forward to inspect the giant plant – and to nibble it. "It's not just amazing, it's delicious too!"

"By the seven tangerines of Barky O'Bonk," said Marsh. "What a clever contraption!"

Frankensaur nodded rather smugly. "Yes, it is."

"No wonder your garden is full of plump and prize-winning plants," said Teggs.

"And if you had more power," Arx suggested, "you could transmit them over large distances."

"Think of it!" Gipsy's eyes took on a faraway look. "With lots of MATTA machines you could send masses of fresh food to needy dinosaurs anywhere in the Jurassic Quadrant."

Arx nodded happily. "Starvation will be a thing of the past."

But Frankensaur looked grave. "Speaking of starvation, where's IGOR with our refreshments?" He turned and left the room. "I must go and check—"

Just then Gipsy's communicator beeped. "Hello?" A few moments later, she gasped. "OK . . . Thanks for the info, Sprite."

"What is it, Gipsy?" asked Teggs.

"DSS HQ have gone through their records and identified our two-headed hijacker," she began. "It's a red spinosaurus bank robber called Jack Spallack – and it's also a green allosaurus thief called Rojan Barb . . ."

Gipsy nodded grimly. "That's right, Captain. It wasn't just one carnivore criminal you talked to on the *Sauropod*, it was *two* of them – squashed together!"

Chapter Five

HEADLESS HORROR

"Two meat-munching crooks," Teggs breathed, "combined into one to make a *super*-carnivore criminal . . ."

"Sounds to me like they've been put through Frankensaur's MATTA whatsit," said Iggy.

Marsh nodded. "And someone could've used this gadget to transmit that big wedge of pumpkin into the side of *Zeta Three* too."

"No," said Arx firmly, looking up from the MATTA machine. "I've just checked the DNA-fusion matrix. This thing can only combine plants with other plants – it simply couldn't work on dinosaurs or metal."

"Well, something certainly did," said Teggs. "Frankensaur told us that Professor Hydra was working on a similar invention, remember? Maybe he's got a machine that can mix and transmit flesh or metal?"

"And it can't be coincidence that our two-headed friend landed here," said Gipsy. "Perhaps they want to get rid of Frankensaur and his machine, so only meat-eaters have this power."

"Hey, look!" Iggy pointed through the window. "There in the old village . . . I saw something move."

Teggs was at the window in an instant. "What was it?"

"It was too dark to tell," said Iggy.

"We'd better check it out," said Teggs. "Gipsy, Marsh, you stay here – make sure that Frankensaur's safe and the castle is secure. Arx, Iggy – come with me!"

The three astrosaurs raced from the room and thundered down the stairs.

Gipsy heard a creak and a slam from the heavy front door as they raced out into the night. *SHUNK! THUNK!* The door was bolted again behind them.

Moments later, IGOR's metallic feet were thumping up the stairs. The hunchbacked robot clanked across the landing with a tray of steaming swamp coffee and crumpets. "I have brought refreshments."

"And by the beard of Nompton, not a moment too soon." Marsh grabbed a mug of the whiffy brew and swigged deeply. "Ahhhh!"

IGOR turned to Gipsy. "Where have your friends gone?"

"Outside, looking for trouble," Gipsy told him, sipping from a mug herself. "While they're away, Marsh and I are going to check out this old castle to make sure it's safe."

"Not necessary," snapped IGOR. "I am here to protect Doctor Frankensaur."

"But you can't be everywhere at once," Gipsy pointed out. "I mean, where is Frankensaur right now?"

"He is . . . resting downstairs." IGOR sounded slightly shifty. "His arm was hurting him."

"He seemed all right a minute ago." Marsh put his empty mug back on the tray. "Gipsy, shall I check he's OK?"

"Good idea," she replied.

IGOR watched him leave, but Gipsy's attention had been taken by a set of wires snaking from the top of the MATTA machine into the ceiling. "Where do those cables lead?" she asked.

"They connect the MATTA machine to a special generator upstairs that gives power to the whole castle," explained IGOR.

"Then that's the first room we should check." Gipsy eyed the lightbulb glowing feebly in the ceiling. "If an intruder cut the power we'd be left in the dark – and at their mercy."

"Hey, Gipsy!" Marsh came trudging back up the stairs. "I can't find Frankensaur anywhere—"

SCRRR-BAMM! A splintering, smashing noise from upstairs made Gipsy jump. "What was that?"

"I don't know," said Marsh gravely. "But I suppose we should find out . . ."

"Come on!" Gipsy raced up the stairs.

"I shall accompany you," IGOR announced.

Within seconds, Gipsy had reached the gloomy upper landing. She fumbled for a light-switch. At the far end of the passage, a door had been smashed open. A dark, misshapen figure came stumbling out.

"Who's there?" Gipsy demanded as Marsh and IGOR arrived beside her.

The robot hit the lights, and in the eerie flickering glow a nightmare monster stood revealed. Its body was broad and dark with white stripes, and it had a thick snaking tail. It walked upright on two powerful legs. One arm stuck out from its side, ending in fearsome claws, while another, bigger arm grew out of its back. But the most petrifying part of its appearance was something at the top of its neck . . .

Or, rather, *nothing* at the top of its neck.

The creature had no head!

"That's impossible," Gipsy whispered as terror squeezed her heart. "Grab it," she told IGOR. "Use those electric ropes of yours!"

"I am programmed only to arrest intruders," said IGOR calmly.

"What do you think that thing is?" Marsh shouted. "Frankensaur's mum come round for tea?"

IGOR ignored him and gave a small bow to the headless monster. "Please, sir, may I fetch you some swamp coffee?"

The weird creature's stomach gave a rumble like a battle cry – and suddenly it thundered down the passage towards Gipsy, IGOR and Marsh at amazing speed.

WHUMP! It kicked Gipsy into IGOR. She fell against the robot with such force that he toppled over the banisters and fell – smashing to pieces in the hallway far below!

"Now look what you did," Gipsy

told the headless monster, ducking as it swiped at her head.

"By the berries of Bingle!" Marsh tried to clobber the body with his hefty tail, but it blocked the blow with its arm and booted him clear across the landing. "*Whoaaaa!*" Cartwheeling out of control, he smashed straight  through a large plate-glass window!

"No!" Gipsy yelled helplessly, as the pilot's screams ended swiftly with a very loud *SPLAT*.

"Hang on, Marsh, I'm coming!" She dodged past the headless horror and sprinted over to the broken window. But the garden outside was dark and rain-lashed, and she could see only shifting shadows. "Where are you?"

58

The thump of heavy footsteps told her exactly where the *monster* was — it was closing on her fast. Gipsy leaned out of the window, grabbed hold of a drainpipe and hoped it would support her weight. As the monster reached out for her with its single hand, she swung herself out of reach and — "*Wheeee!*" — quickly slid down the pipe, tearing ivy from the wall as she went.

While the monster stamped its feet on the landing in helpless fury, Gipsy looked around for Marsh. In a flash of lightning, she suddenly saw him lying sprawled inside the largest pumpkin she had ever seen. Luckily he was still breathing – he was only knocked out. Half of the squash had been well and truly squashed by his bulky armoured body; it had broken his fall and saved his life.

But as more lightning lit up the night sky, Gipsy realized that the other half of the pumpkin was metal – a huge sheet of solid steel with words written in big green letters: *ZETA THREE*.

"That's been taken from the side of the star-vault," she breathed. "So there really *is* a machine that can mix metal and plants together."

Suddenly Gipsy heard movement behind her. She whirled round, hooves raised and ready, heart pounding. "Who's there?" she hissed into the night as the sound of dragging footsteps on the grass drew closer. "*Who's there . . . ?*"

Chapter Six

HEADS AND TALES

Gipsy gulped, spooked out to the max as the footsteps came closer still . . .

Finally, by the light of a passing meteor, she recognized Dr Frankensaur stumbling towards her — and breathed a sigh of relief. He was clutching his injured arm and waving his bandaged tail, and looked quite unwell.

"Gipsy," he whispered. "I . . . I'm so glad you're all right."

"Where've you been, Frankensaur?" she demanded. "Did

you know there's a mad monster running around your landing – and half-
metal veggies growing in your garden? Just what is going on around here?"

"It's IGOR. He's gone haywire." Frankensaur's voice sounded strangely lifeless. "When I went downstairs, he attacked me and tied me up – I've only just got free."

"Haywire is right," said Gipsy. "Well, don't worry about IGOR – he's broken to bits now."

Frankensaur did not react. "IGOR carried the plans of my MATTA machine in his memory banks – he must've shared them with the meat-eaters!" He turned back to the castle. "Come inside. I have found some old weapons that might hold off the headless intruder, but I am not sure how to use them."

"OK. Let's go." Deciding that Marsh was probably safer in the pumpkin, Gipsy followed Frankensaur through a side door into the castle . . .

Soaked and cold, unaware of the danger their friends were facing, Teggs led Arx and Iggy along the treacherous trail to the old village. The path snaked in and out of gulleys and up and down crags and cliffs. Iggy sighed. "Whatever I saw, it's probably miles away by now."

"Well, we should have a good view
of the village from the top of this hill,"
said Teggs. "We can spy out the land."
He spotted some pointy purple weeds
growing through the rocks and smiled.
"But first, a quick snack—"

"Captain, don't!" said Arx urgently.
"Those look like narg-nettles – super-
rare and not at all nice."

"I read about those things," said Iggy.
"The more they prickle, the faster they
grow. Somehow they detect anyone
trying to eat them and give them a sting."

"Yuk!" Teggs stuck out
his tongue – and the
narg-nettle stretched
up and stung it! "*OW!*
Forget the snack – and
watch where you step."

They continued to
the summit. On the
other side of the hill was
a steep path leading to the ruins of the

old village they'd spied from the shuttle. There was no movement, no sign of life.

"Hey, look." Arx pointed into the valley. "There's something gleaming down there."

Teggs set off along the path. "Let's check it out."

The gleaming thing turned out to be a large metal cube. "It's a portable cooker," said Arx. "And it looks new."

"Someone has been camping out here." Teggs nudged aside a slab of stone to reveal a dirty plastic crate. "Look at this empty tub of diplodocus burgers.

Urgh! The 'best before' date was only a few weeks ago."

"There's more camping stuff in here," Iggy called from inside the nearest hut. "And some papers . . ." He came out looking grim. "Photos of Frankensaur's castle – and a plan of the different floors, with possible ways in . . ."

"And while you're busy making discoveries," came a gruff snarl from behind them, "guess what? You've been lured here from the castle – right where we want you."

Teggs spun round to find a familiar two-headed, two-tailed monster striding out from behind a ruined building – with a large white gun cradled in three of his four arms.

"So it was *you* I spotted," said Iggy. "Our hijacker friends – Jack Spallack and Rojan Barb!"

Rojan's green face smiled nastily. "So. You know who we are."

"Or who you *were*, anyway," said Arx. "Before you were turned into a monster."

Jack frowned. "But Professor Hydra will make us normal again once he's finished his experiments. He promised."

"Shut up!" said Rojan crossly.

"Hydra," breathed Teggs. "The

carnivore genius that Frankensaur told us about."

"Where is Hydra now?" Iggy looked around.

"He *was* camping out in these old ruins with the rest of us," said Jack. "But for the last few weeks he's been working hard – inside the castle!"

Iggy gasped. "INSIDE?"

"You're such a blabber-mouth," groaned Rojan.

"Guys, we've left Gipsy, Marsh and Frankensaur in terrible danger." Teggs raised his communicator to his mouth. "We must warn them."

"Forget it!" snarled Rojan, as he and Jack jabbed the gun in the astrosaurs' direction. "Professor Hydra's got plans for you!"

★

69

Back on the ground floor of the castle, Gipsy was following Frankensaur along a dark corridor. "Is that monster still upstairs?" she whispered.

"I don't know," said Frankensaur slowly. "IGOR left me tied up in the  living room. I heard that headless body crashing about on the landing. Maybe it knew you were going to search the castle and find its hidden lair . . ."

"So it attacked first," Gipsy reasoned. "Makes sense."

"Anyway . . . I heard the window break. As soon as I untied my ropes, I ran outside to find you." He headed towards a large door at the end of the passage. "Come on – the weapons are in this storeroom . . ."

"Hang on a moment." Gipsy held back, nodding to the doctor's broken arm in its plaster cast. "You undid the knots with just one hand?"

"Er . . ." Frankensaur looked shifty. "I mean I *chewed* through the ropes. Now, quickly, before the headless thing finds us."

"Hang on *another* moment." Gipsy narrowed her eyes. "If you haven't seen this monster, Frankensaur . . . *how did you know it has no head*?"

SLAM! The door was kicked open from the other side to reveal the headless stripy

thing standing there, clawed hand
clutching blindly, tail sweeping from side
to side.

Horrified, Gipsy turned to run – but
Frankensaur lashed out with his tail
and tripped her up. She twisted round
and landed on her back – but before
she could rise, the creepy creature had
stomped out of the storeroom and
planted one big foot on her tummy,
pinning her in place.

"Frankensaur," she gasped. "You tricked me!"

"Don't blame the poor doctor," came a muffled voice from somewhere close by. "He is not responsible for his actions . . ."

As Gipsy watched, incredulous, Frankensaur stiffly pulled off his plaster cast to reveal an unharmed arm that was striped black and white – a perfect replacement for the monster's mis-matched limb.

"And now, I shall reveal to you the *real* genius around here!" came the muffled voice again. "Observe . . ."

Frankensaur began to peel the bandages off the lump at the end of his tail. With a shiver of terror, Gipsy realized that this was where the voice had come from.

That was no simple injury at the tip of Frankensaur's tail – it was a HEAD! The head of a fierce carnivore, bandaged up purely to hide it from sight. And from its shape and size, it looked like the very same head that the monster holding Gipsy was missing.

"You are right to be afraid, my dear." The head at the end of the tail smiled nastily. "My name is Professor Hydra. I am in complete control of Doctor Frankensaur. And thanks to our combined genius, meat-eating dinosaurs will soon control the galaxy!"

Chapter Seven

THE MONSTERS' POWER

Marched at gunpoint through the crumbling servants' village, Teggs searched around helplessly for some way of escape. He knew that both Arx and Iggy beside him were thinking the same thing – they had to get back to the castle and help Gipsy.

If only I could call her on the communicator, Teggs thought. But Rojan-Jack was following close behind them and looked ready to fire his gun at any moment.

"Does Frankensaur know this Hydra character is hiding in his castle?" he demanded.

"Better than that," Jack chortled.

"Hydra's hiding in Frankensaur's body!"

The news stopped Teggs, Arx and Iggy in their tracks. "*What?*"

"Frankensaur's 'injuries' are a bit more serious than you thought." Rojan grinned. "He's got Hydra's head hidden on the end of his tail – controlling his whole body."

"Another mutant misfit," sighed Arx. "Just like you."

"Keep moving!" Jack snarled.

Moving off again with Teggs and Arx, Iggy glowered at their two-headed captor. "If Hydra is back at the castle, why does he want us over here?"

"You'll see," said Rojan. "Once he's linked Frankensaur's MATTA machine to his own *MAMMMA* machine."

"MAMMMA?" Arx echoed.

"Yeah, you might well call for your mama," jeered Jack.

"He wasn't calling for his mama," said Rojan wearily. "He was asking what MAMMMA stands for."

Jack thought hard. "She stands to reach something from the top shelf—"

"Will you SHUT UP!" Rojan snapped. "MAMMMA stands for Mix And Mangle Metal/Meaty Areas."

Iggy gasped. "So that's how you two got mixed up together – and how you mangled *Zeta Three*'s metal walls and weapons."

"Right," Rojan agreed, "with a little help from Frankensaur's planty version. The boss is running them both as one mega-MATTA-MAMMMA machine."

"But that would require massive amounts of power," said Arx, puzzled. "The old castle generator can't be strong enough."

"It isn't." Rojan smiled craftily. "See that ruin in front of you? It's a parking spot for our spaceship, which has all the extra power Hydra needs . . ."

Teggs peered at the remains of a long roofless building, apparently filled with timber and straw – and saw steel glinting beneath. "Disguised," he breathed. "So we couldn't spot it from above."

"Correct." Rojan pulled a remote control from the rags of his outfit and pressed a button. The hidden ship began to hum with energy.

Iggy glared as the straw fell away to reveal more of the vessel beneath. "I suppose your friends travelled straight back here after dropping you off beside Marsh's spaceship."

"Right," Rojan agreed. "A star-vault passing by in local space was too good a test for the MATTA-MAMMMA machine. One of the toughest ships ever – and I just space-walked across and kicked my way inside. Shame it wasn't loaded with goodies, but next time—"

"Uh-oh!" Jack sniffed and blinked, his nostrils twitching. "I'm going to sneeze."

"Don't you dare," growled Rojan. "Cover your nose, Jack! Look the other way—"

"*AAACHOOOOOOO!*" The sneeze exploded out of Jack's red nose and sprayed over Rojan's face!

"*URRRGH!*" Rojan groaned.

While the carnivores were distracted, Teggs thwacked a lump of rubble with his tail like a cricketer hitting a ball. *SMACK!* It hit Rojan on the forehead and he dropped the gun.

"Come on!" Teggs ran off, reaching for his communicator. "We've got to warn Gipsy . . ."

But then a giant creature loomed out of the dark ahead of them. It was a huge scaly blob with five snarling faces in its middle. It walked on ten little arms, and as many meaty tails and legs waved from its top like tentacles.

Iggy gasped. "What a monster!"

"How dare you!" the creature rasped, bobbing as it advanced. "We're Bim-Wim-Lim-Dim-Ponko – five friends combined into one."

"And five times as revolting," muttered Teggs. "Back the way we came!" But too late he saw that Rojan-Jack had recovered, and was pointing the gun straight at them.

ZUMMM! A red ray transfixed the astrosaurs. Teggs tried to move, but found that he was helpless, as stiff as a statue.

"Nice shot, Rojan-Jack," said the blob-monster. "The freeze-ray will hold them till the boss is through with them."

Rojan-Jack nodded both heads.

"About time you showed your faces.
Have you finished setting up the
lightning converter?"

"Yep." Bim-Wim-Lim-Dim-Ponko
smiled. "It's right on top of that hill, like
Hydra wanted."

Teggs strained to see to the top of the
nearest hill. A metal spike was pointing
up at the clouds; lightning seemed drawn
to it, striking it again and again.

"Must be a three-stage process," Arx
said through stiff lips. "First, the converter
gathers electrical energy. Second, it

feeds it through to a booster in the spaceship—"

"And third, it zaps the energy over to the castle," said Bim-Wim-Lim-Dim-Ponko, plugging a fat cable into a satellite dish sticking out of their craft. "With the extra power, the boss's operation can go ahead at last . . ."

Operation? Teggs could only watch helplessly as the gloating carnivores grinned with delight at the thought of what was to come . . .

Over in Frankensaur's castle, Gipsy was being dragged up the stairs by the headless-body beast. Frankensaur plodded ahead of them. But it was the head on his tail – Professor Hydra's head – that was clearly in control.

"Let me get this straight," growled Gipsy. "When Frankensaur spoke to us all before – that was really *you*, making his head talk?"

Frankensaur's head suddenly swung round to face her. "That's right," he said slowly. "Professor Hydra is the cleverest daspletosaurus there ever was. Brighter than Attila the Atrocious! Brainier than Omarg the Mean!"

"Why, thank you," said Hydra's head with a horrible smile.

"Losing your head doesn't seem very bright." Gipsy struggled in the monster's grip. "How does your real body even know where to go?"

"I am steering it by remote control," Hydra revealed. "A small circuit on the back of my neck picks up my thoughts."

"So you're controlling that thing *and* poor Doctor Frankensaur," Gipsy realized. "But Rojan and Jack have two heads in one body too – and both of them can talk. Why didn't Frankensaur try to warn us?"

"Rojan and Jack are both rather dim, so neither can control the other." Hydra smiled smugly. "Frankensaur and I are both geniuses – but my will is stronger than his. And because we are linked, all the knowledge in his head is now in *my* head too!" As they reached the top landing, he signalled his body to stop moving, and bobbed closer to Gipsy. "For many years I have been working on my Mix And Mangle Metal/Meaty Areas machine. I plan to create the ultimate living weapon – a creature made from the nastiest parts of a dozen carnivore breeds *and* their space armour."

"You mean, like the head of a T. rex on

the armoured body of a megalosaurus with the claws of a raptor?" Gipsy shivered in the grip of her captor. "That's horrible."

"Thank you," growled Hydra. "Unfortunately, I could not control how the different dinosaurs were mixed together. My test subject volunteers became messed-up mutants . . ."

Gipsy nodded. "Like Rojan-Jack."

"So I tracked Frankensaur to this castle," Hydra went on. "When our spaceship landed, the doctor sent IGOR to investigate . . ."

"And you caught the poor robot and reprogrammed him, I suppose," said Gipsy.

"With IGOR's help it was child's play to capture this fool." Hydra's head looked snootily at the body that supported him.

"But as I demonstrated my MAMMMA machine to him, he tried to escape. I stopped him, but in the process we both blundered into the combining ray . . ."

"And that's how you became a monster," Gipsy realized.

"A lucky accident, as it turned out." Hydra nodded to the broken door on the landing. "Now that Frankensaur's mind is linked to mine, I can think bigger than ever! Take a look . . ."

The headless body dragged Gipsy over to the shattered doorway. Inside was a big rusty generator, humming with power – hooked up to a powerful-looking black machine.

A small TV screen was set into it, and
Gipsy could see Teggs, Arx and Iggy
standing frozen to the spot beside a
spaceship.

"What have you done to my friends?"
she demanded.

"It's what I'm *going* to do to them that
should concern you." Hydra threw back
his head – there was nothing much else
he *could* throw – and laughed. "Once
I send the signal to my servants, my
ultimate experiment can finally begin!"

Chapter Eight

MONSTER MADNESS!

In the village, still frozen beside Arx and Iggy, Teggs could see Frankensaur's castle in the distance. "Oh, Gipsy," he murmured sadly. "I hope you're not in as much trouble as we are!"

Suddenly three flashes of light shone at one of the tower windows.

"That's Hydra's signal," said Bim-Wim-Lim-Dim-Ponko, pointing a remote at the lightning converter. "Feeding through the power – now!"

The giant spike crackled with energy. Sparks shot out from the satellite dish and it glowed bright green.

Both Rojan-Jack's heads spoke as one:

"Now to beam the power to the castle, where Hydra's machines will pick it up – and send a super-strong MATTA-MAMMMA ray back over here . . ."

The light zapped over to the castle in a glittering stream, and Bim–Wim–Lim–Dim–Ponko laughed. "Here comes your operation, astrosaurs!"

Ka-SHROWWW! A glaring, flaring beam of power engulfed Teggs, Arx and Iggy. A sizzling sensation seared through Teggs's bones. It felt as though something were pulling him inside out. He groaned and gasped. Flashes of

colour danced before his eyes.

Then the beam cut out. Teggs collapsed to the ground, and his friends fell beside him. He felt dizzy and sore all over.

"Ha, ha!" Bim-Wim-Lim-Dim-Ponko pointed its many tails and laughed. "Just look at those astro-suckers now."

"These freaky knuckleheads won't be laughing by the time I'm through with them." Iggy bunched his fists – then boggled his eyes. "Oh, no – look! My claws! My thumb-spikes!" His voice dropped to a shocked whisper. "They . . . they've turned into . . ."

"*Onions?*" Teggs's mouth fell open in astonishment. "No way! It's one thing to turn spaceship walls into pumpkins, but *this* . . ."

He turned angrily to face Rojan-Jack and thwacked his tail against the ground. But instead of a solid *THUMP* he heard only a limp *swoosh!* He couldn't feel his tail at all.

"Captain," squeaked Iggy, pointing an onion finger in disbelief. "Your tail . . . it's turned into a BABY TREE!"

"What?" Teggs looked behind him and did a double take. His big spiky, power-packed tail had gone, to be replaced by the leafy branches of a small sapling. "I don't believe it! This can't be happening . . ."

"Well, it is," jeered Bim-Wim-Lim-Dim-Ponko. "What are you going to do, Captain – sweep the floor with that big bad tail of yours?"

"Laugh while you can," said Arx, getting woozily to his feet. "I've still got my horns. They will sort you out!"

"But, Arx, you *don't* still have your horns." Teggs gulped. "Your whole head-frill has gone."

Iggy nodded, horror-struck. "It's turned into a big lily pad with cactuses poking out!"

"Our toughest attack parts have been taken away!" Arx was going boss-eyed trying to see his new leafy head-frill. "But what has become of them?"

Back in Frankensaur's castle, the
MAMMMA machine juddered to a
stop. Gipsy's eyes were on stalks as she
watched her friends and their unlikely
plant-parts on the little TV screen.

"What have you done, Hydra?" she
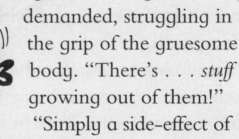 demanded, struggling in
the grip of the gruesome
body. "There's . . . *stuff*
growing out of them!"
"Simply a side-effect of
combining my flesh-mangling
MAMMMA machine with
Frankensaur's veggie version –
whatever I take is replaced by plant-life."
The professor's horrible head bobbed
about excitedly at the end of the tail. "But
who cares about that? The *real* experiment
should be coming to an end downstairs.
Let's go and see. Come on – quickly!"

Hydra steered Frankensaur's body out
onto the landing and down the creaky

steps. Gipsy gasped as
her headless captor
carried her away in
pursuit.

By the time
they arrived in
Frankensaur's lab,
the white MATTA
machine was whirring,
and something strange and sinister was
forming in the cubicle. It was like some
kind of giant snake, twice as big as
Gipsy, with a large, shield-shaped head,
its squirming body covered in purple
prickles and ivory spikes. Huge slabs of
metal armour added to its bulk.

With horror, Gipsy realized that she
was looking at a super-sized version of
Teggs's tail, with Arx's horns and bony
head-frill perched on top, and Iggy's stun
claws and thumb-spikes — much enlarged
— wriggling like sharp legs beneath it!

"That's revolting . . ." she whispered.

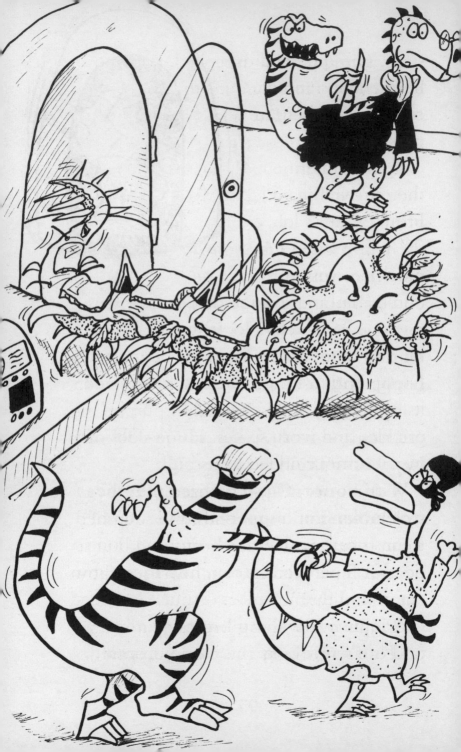

"It is *genius*," Hydra replied, bobbing forward on Frankensaur's tail to study the creature. "I have mixed, transmitted and transmogrified matter — and created new life!"

Gipsy pressed a button on her communicator. She couldn't risk talking to Teggs, but she could at least let him know she was alive by allowing him to listen in on what was happening . . .

Hydra was still burbling on. "Since my monster is part Teggs, part Arx and part Iggy, I shall call it — *Tarxig!*"

"I don't get it!" Gipsy cried. "You've stolen bits from my friends and squashed them together to make a monster, but it doesn't have a brain or a heart — so how *can* it be alive?"

"Plants live without brains or a heart, and are sensitive to the world around them," Hydra informed her. "The flesh here has been combined with narg-nettles – and the more narg-nettles sting, the faster they grow."

Gipsy understood now. "So that's why you needed Frankensaur's plant-mashing machine as well as your flesh-and-metal mixing version."

Tarxig suddenly whipped forward, like a cobra trying to strike, and Hydra jerked his head away. "Ha! See that? Tarxig has absorbed the instinct of the narg-nettles. He cannot see, but he can detect vibrations, just as the nettles can. He *wants* to attack, to grow even bigger and even stronger . . ."

"A living weapon . . ." Gipsy stared at the monstrous mish-mash as it scuttled out of the cubicle on its claws, peering about blindly. "You think you can conquer the entire Vegetarian Sector with things like this?"

"Of course!" Hydra beamed. "Once the MATTA-MAMMMA machine is perfected, I can target the dinosaurs of an entire planet, remove their toughest parts, and turn the pieces into monsters that will attack their owners! And meantime, we invade . . ."

"Knowing they'll be too busy battling

their own body-bits to fight you." Gipsy struggled in the grip of Hydra's brainless body as Tarxig slithered closer. "But you won't win, Hydra – the DSS will send spaceships to destroy you."

"Are you forgetting what I did to your friend's star-vault? My mighty machine can mess up metal as well. I will turn the walls of your mightiest battleships into lettuce leaves! I will transform DSS HQ into a pile of cabbage in space!" Hydra sniggered. "The Vegetarian Sector will be defenceless – and the entire Carnivore Sector will worship me as their supreme ruler!"

As Hydra laughed madly, the twitching Tarxig held still for a

 moment as if scenting the air – then lunged for Gipsy. Desperately, just in time, she twisted free of the arm that held her and ran out onto the landing.

But Hydra's headless body kicked the tail-beast after her.

"Run, Gipsy!" Hydra shouted. "Let's see how far you get before my creature catches you. One thump from those spikes and prickles, and you will be dead!"

Gipsy heard his shouts echo through the castle. "Captain!" she cried into her communicator. "I hope you and Arx and Iggy are all right . . . but I don't think *I* will be for much longer!"

Behind her, she could hear the thump and slither of the pursuing Tarxig . . .

Chapter Nine

TEARS AND TRICKERY

Teggs gulped as Gipsy's voice burst from his communicator. He, Arx and Iggy had been listening gravely as the astounding situation unfolded – and so too had Rojan-Jack and Bim-Wim-Lim-Dim-Ponko.

"Well," said Teggs to his foes. "It doesn't sound to me as if putting your bodies back to normal is high on Hydra's 'to do' list."

"We'll see about that," Rojan growled. He went into the spaceship and came out a few moments later with a silver

hover-scooter.
"Bim-Wim-Lim-
Dim-Ponko – stay
here and guard the
prisoners. I'm going
back to the castle to
talk to the boss."

"Me too!" said Jack,
a bit pointlessly.

Teggs watched the two-headed
monster whizz away, then turned to Arx
and Iggy. "Somehow, we've got to reach
the castle and help Gipsy."

Iggy stared sadly at his onion claws.
"But how can we get past a dirty great
monster like that when we've been
turned part plant?"

"Answer: you can't," jeered Bim-Wim-
Lim-Dim-Ponko. "What are you going
to do – cry about it?"

"Astrosaurs never give up," said Arx
defiantly.

"But crying's a good idea," Teggs

murmured, "so long as *we're* not the ones who are weeping." He nodded at Iggy's onion fingers. "Ig, if you were to scratch your thumb-spikes on a narg-nettle . . ."

Iggy spied a clump of the purple plants close by and suddenly got what his captain was driving at. "Hold your breath, guys!" he whispered – and slowly reached out to grasp the nettles. The sharp prickles cut through the brown onion skins and into the glistening vegetables inside. "Can't feel a thing!" he assured them. "But as for Bim and company . . ."

"Hey . . ." As the raw onion fumes carried to them, Bim-Wim-Lim-Dim-Ponko's eyes began to water and run. "What's going on?" They tried to wipe their eyes and noses with their tails, but only managed to slap themselves in the face.

"It's working!" hissed Arx excitedly. "The onions are making them cry, and

104

they can't see through their tears."

"And now I'll give them something
to *really* cry about . . ." Teggs curled his
springy sapling tail around a bunch of
narg-nettles, uprooted them — and then
shoved them into the monster's faces!

"*ARRRGH!*" A chorus of howls went
up. Teggs nipped behind Bim–Wim–Lim–
Dim–Ponko and gave the mutant a hefty
shove. *WHUMP!* It fell over.

"Now it's my turn!" Arx rushed forward

with his cactus
horns and jabbed
the beast on its
bottom. With
a raging howl,
Bim-Wim-Lim-
Dim-Ponko
jumped straight
up into the air,
flipped over, and
landed on a sharp rock.

KRACKK!

The multiple-monster was out cold.

Teggs gave his friends a crooked smile.
"Not too shabby for three dinosaurs
recovering from an operation!" Then
he spoke into his
communicator.
"Gipsy, this is
Teggs. We've
escaped!
Are you all
right?"

"Oh, Captain!" Gipsy's voice crackled from the communicator. "Between your tail, Arx's horns, Iggy's claws and a bunch of nettles, I don't know how much longer I can hold out."

"You must," Teggs urged her. "We're on our way to get you – but so is Rojan-Jack, and he's way ahead of us."

Gipsy groaned. "That's all I need!"

"We'll be there as fast as we can," Teggs promised.

Arx pointed to the carnivores' spaceship. "That's the quickest way."

"But can I fly it with onions for fingers?" Iggy rushed inside. "Guess there's only one way to find out!"

In Frankensaur's gloomy castle, Gipsy was racing down the stairs towards the hallway. She could hear Tarxig scrabbling after her like some mutant scorpion.

Suddenly, a step gave way beneath her

and her hoof crashed through the rotting
wood. Gasping with surprise, she heard
the heavy *whoosh* of Tarxig as he jumped
over her shoulder. Had she not fallen, he
would've smashed into her back!

Instead, the living tail-beast dropped
onto the shiny form of IGOR, who still
lay broken at the bottom of the staircase.
Ka-CLANG! The robot twitched under
the impact, his hand clenching and
unclenching. Confused, Tarxig began

to hammer the robot with horns, spikes and leaves, denting the tough casing and causing sparks to burst from within.

"You two deserve each other," Gipsy muttered. Slowly, carefully, she pulled her leg free of the splintered stair and crept down to the hallway. If she could just make it to the pumpkin patch, wake up Marsh and get back to her friends . . .

Gipsy reached the big front door and pulled back the bolts.

But then the door was kicked open — and in a flash of lightning, she saw the nightmare shape of Rojan-Jack framed in the doorway.

"Going somewhere, girlie?" Rojan growled as Jack bared his teeth in a nasty grin. "I don't think so . . ."

Gipsy heard more scuttling behind her. Frantically she tried to shove the two-headed terror aside – but three of his arms grabbed her. "Get out of the way!" she shouted, struggling to move. "You don't understand the danger . . ."

Looking back, her eyes widened as Tarxig scrabbled across the hallway towards them – spikes and horns gleaming, leaves rustling, ready to jump and deliver the killing blow . . .

But suddenly a steel cord lashed out from the far end of the hall – and wrapped itself tightly about the tail-beast's middle before it could attack. Tarxig strained and pulled like a mad dog on a leash, but could get no closer to the door – as a slightly crumpled metal figure was holding on tight . . .

"IGOR!" Gipsy exclaimed. "You stopped that thing!"

"Tail mutant . . . is not . . . recognized as . . . a guest," IGOR croaked, his head sinking back to the floor.

"But *I* am," said Rojan, gripping Gipsy even tighter. "And I'm going to have a word with Professor Hydra."

"Maybe even *two* words," added Jack. "Like 'good' and 'evening'! Or 'hello' and 'hello'. Er, does that count as two words or is it just one repeated—?"

"SHUT UP!" roared Rojan. "If Hydra doesn't split us apart soon, I'll go crazy! I'll go—"

BONG! CLANG! The sound of two metallic wallops rang out. As Rojan-Jack slid to the floor, Gipsy saw a figure wielding a massive spade behind him . . .

"There!" it told the sprawling body. "*That's* for kicking me off my ship!"

"Pilot Marsh!" Gipsy sighed with relief and gave him a hug. "Wow, am I ever glad to see you!"

"By the nibbled nose of the purple pish, it's good to see you too!" Marsh frowned when he saw the twitching Tarxig on its steel lead, and IGOR feebly twitching on the floor beside it. "But it's not so good to see *those* things. What in the seven numps of Bingbong has been happening around here?"

"You'll never believe me," said Gipsy. "Come on. We've got to get out of here and—"

"No!" Frankensaur thundered into the hall – Hydra's head waving about on the end of his tail and a laser pistol clutched in his clawed hand. "Close and bolt that door, Marsh – or I'll shoot Gipsy!"

Marsh boggled at the sight of the monstrous scientist. "I wish I'd stayed in that pumpkin now!" Slowly, shakily, he turned and obeyed.

"Thank you," purred Hydra. He fired at the thick wire that held his creation prisoner, snapping it in two. Tarxig wriggled with pleasure as it shook the steel away. "Now, my test can continue – with *two* subjects. Prepare to die!"

Chapter Ten

CASTLE CARNAGE!

Gipsy gulped. Her heart was banging so hard against her ribs, she guessed Tarxig could sense the vibrations a mile away. It scuttled towards them, spikes shaking, horns glinting, ready to strike—

But something else struck first – at the castle itself!

WHA-BOOOOOM! With a gigantic explosion, the wall smashed apart in a storm of stone and cement. Gipsy and Marsh were thrown to the floor. Frankensaur and Hydra's head were half buried in rubble. Debris rained down and dust turned the air to a choking fog.

"By the fourteen fangs of Fobrob the Fink," Marsh groaned as the echoes of the blast faded and the air began to clear. "What was that?"

Coughing and gasping, Gipsy got up – and almost bumped her head on the nose-cone of a massive rocket, which was poking through the wall. "It was this thing! But where did it come from?"

"Sorry about that slight crash-landing, everyone!" A large orange-brown figure came striding through the smoke. "Flying a strange spaceship's not so easy when your pilot's hands have turned to onions . . ."

"Captain Teggs!" Gipsy hugged him tight. "I've been so worried."

"So have we," said Arx, emerging from the side of the spaceship, his lily-pad head-frill waving in the smoke and his cactuses a-tremble. "We saw Rojan-Jack's scooter outside. Where is he?"

"Er, I think you're standing on him, Arx," said Iggy, scrambling out to join them. Sure enough, two dazed faces were sticking out of the debris. "Poor old Rojan-Jack. He'll have a couple of headaches after that!"

Gipsy ran over to embrace Arx and Iggy. "I saw what happened to you all. You poor things, just look at you . . ."

Marsh scratched his head. "I wish I knew what was going on around here!"

But before anyone could explain, the stones beside him erupted – and the thrashing, spiky menace of Tarxig appeared, swiping viciously this way and that. It seemed to sense Teggs close by and reared up to attack . . .

"How dare you!" Teggs bellowed. "May I remind you that at least three-quarters of your body belongs to members of the Dinosaur Space Service, and that I am your captain? You're a disgrace!"

Tarxig cringed and shied away. It was almost as if it could hear and understand Teggs's words.

"We order you not to harm another living thing," Arx shouted.

"Now, SIT!" said Iggy sternly.

Tarxig curled up sulkily on the stony carpet, and lay still.

"I don't believe it!" Gipsy stared, incredulous. "How did that work? Tarxig's got no ears."

"True – but it was built from our bodies," Arx reminded her. "And our bodies are used to doing what we tell them to!"

"Well, now you will do as *I* tell you," came a voice from the other end of the hallway – as Hydra's head emerged from the rubble.

"So you're Professor Hydra." Teggs waved his sapling tail crossly. "I have a bone to pick with you – well, a small tree actually."

"Your threats are meaningless." Hydra pointed his pistol at Teggs. "If I can no

 longer use you in my tests, I shall kill you all where you stand!"

But suddenly his hand began to twitch and shake – until he was pointing the gun at himself! "No!" he squeaked. "What's happening?"

"How do you like it?" boomed a familiar voice – the voice of Dr Frankensaur, lifting his own dusty head from the wreckage. "All this time you've been controlling me – making me say your words, steering me around. I've been a prisoner in my own body."

He smiled grimly at Hydra. "You
thought you were my master. But I've
been resting, building my strength,
waiting for the best moment to fight
back. And that time has finally come!"

As the astrosaurs watched, amazed,
Frankensaur swung his tail round and
round — throwing Hydra's
head into a spin.
"Stop!" the
carnivore
wailed. "Stop
him, my
body . . ."

The
headless
black-and-
white creature
that had menaced Gipsy and Marsh
reappeared, staggering down the stairs
towards Frankensaur. But without a
moment's pause for thought, Teggs raced
down the hallway and jumped on it,

sending it crashing to the floor. Iggy and Arx quickly joined him on top of the strange beast; though it struggled, it could barely move beneath their weight.

"Thank you, astrosaurs." Frankensaur grunted with effort, spinning his tail even faster. "I'm nearly finished here . . ."

"Nooooo!" moaned Hydra. "Can't think straight . . . can't control you . . . can't—"

BWAMM! Frankensaur thumped the horrid head at the end of his tail against the wall with all his strength. Hydra went cross-eyed and his body jerked beneath Teggs, Arx and Iggy — and was finally still.

"There," said Frankensaur  with a huge sigh of relief. "Hydra is knocked out. I can think for myself again."

"I'm glad to hear it." Teggs beamed. "And I'd be even gladder to hear that you can dismantle Tarxig and put everyone back to normal."

"Of course." Frankensaur nodded. "I know exactly what Hydra did. His thoughts are in my head, just as mine were in his. But I will need extra power – and since the spaceship is smashed and the castle a wreck . . ."

"You can use power from our ship, the *Sauropod*," said Arx. "We'll give you whatever you need."

"Absolutely," Teggs agreed, nibbling a few leaves from the end of his tail. "I'll be glad to be back to normal – but in the meantime, I have to admit I'm quite tasty!"

The day that followed was very busy.

The *Sauropod* landed in the castle's front garden beside the crashed spaceship. Alass, Teggs's security chief, put Tarxig the tail-beast in a cage. Then her team of ankylosaurs arrested Rojan-Jack and Bim-Wim-Lim-Dim-Ponko. Neither put up a fight once they heard that Frankensaur was willing to turn them back to normal.

Marsh helped the *Sauropod*'s engineers, making *Zeta Three* spaceworthy again.

While they worked, Iggy was busy repairing IGOR. The robot was soon better than ever and ready to serve his master once again. In fact, he  helped Arx connect power-lines to the MATTA-MAMMMA machines upstairs so that Frankensaur could use both at once without a hitch. The dimorphodon helped the doctor prepare for the reverse-transplants, lending their beaks to the complicated controls.

"No mad scientist's lab is complete without a few useful dino-birds," Teggs observed with a smile.

"I think we're ready to start," said Frankensaur, studying his tail to make certain that Hydra's head was still fast asleep. "The sooner I'm my own dinosaur again, the better!"

Iggy and Teggs carried Hydra's body into the cubicle, and Frankensaur stood beside it. Arx set up the focus tubes with care. Sprite switched on the MAMMMA machine while Gipsy worked the MATTA one downstairs. Lights and colour flashed and sparked about the lab as the power surged higher and higher . . .

"Let's hope it works," said Iggy, crossing his onions.

With a sudden flare of brilliant light and a hiss of weird energy, both machines shuddered to a stop – revealing Frankensaur now had matching arms and a headless tail! Hydra's bonce was back where it should've been all along, and his body had regained its proper arm.

"Woo-hoo!" Teggs cheered. "You've done it."

"And soon you will all be back to
normal!" said Frankensaur happily.

The doctor was as good as his word.
Tarxig was fetched, and Teggs, Arx and
Iggy were lined up beside it. Gipsy
assisted Frankensaur as he worked,
desperately hoping that the operation
would go smoothly . . .

And it did!

"We're cured!" whooped Teggs. He
danced around and kissed his tail,
then did a can-can with Gipsy and
Arx – whose horns were pointier than
ever. Iggy joined in, once he had given
Frankensaur a long, loud round of
applause with his back-to-normal hands.

As for Tarxig, all that was left of the
curious creature was a pile of nettles, a
few onions, a lily pad, some cactuses and
a large twig.

Woken by the noise of partying,
Hydra opened his eyes. "Ouch! My
head . . . What happened . . . ?"

"You'll have plenty of time to figure
that out, Professor," said Gipsy sweetly.
"Behind bars in a top-security space
prison!"

"Along with your tadpole-brained test
cases," Arx added as Alass brought in
Rojan-Jack and Bim-Wim-Lim-Dim-
Ponko for their treatment.

"Frankensaur will put your bodies

back to normal," said Iggy, "but don't worry about missing each other – you can all share a cell!"

"And what will you do next, Doctor Frankensaur?" asked Teggs. "We'll repair all the damage to your castle, of course . . ."

"No need," said Frankensaur. "Now that you've taken care of Hydra and his friends, I don't have to hide in this

miserable old place any more. IGOR and I will move back to Hadros Major and live somewhere bright and busy again!"

"Cooooool!" said IGOR with an electronic burble. "Can we shack up on a beach near a repair shop, so I can go surfing and check out all the metal mamas?"

Frankensaur chuckled. "Now that IGOR's been rebuilt by Iggy, he seems rather more adventurous!"

"Adventure's what you get with astrosaurs," Teggs agreed happily. "And it's high time we went looking for another one." He winked at his crewmates. "In this crazy universe of ours . . . nothing else MATTAs!"

ASTRO PUZZLE TIME

The Castle of Frankensaur
QUIZ QUESTIONS

Questions:

1. How did Pilot Marsh escape the monster on *Zeta Three*?

2. What refreshments did IGOR bring Marsh and Gipsy?

3. What was under Doctor Frankensaur's tail bandage?

4. Pilot Marsh fell into a pumpkin, but what was half of it made of?

5. What were Teggs's tail, Arx's horns and Iggy's claws turned into?

Answers:

1. In an escape pod
2. Swamp coffee and crumpets
3. Professor Hydra's head
4. A sheet of metal from the side of *Zeta Three*
5. A sapling, a lily pad with cactuses poking out and onions . . . and Tarxig!

ASTRO PUZZLE TIME

The Castle of Frankensaur
WORDSEARCH

C	B	A	D	T	A	I	L	F	S	E	D
R	M	S	P	O	N	G	J	I	A	H	I
U	O	T	Q	R	T	G	T	Z	U	P	M
M	I	E	J	Z	W	Y	A	T	R	S	O
P	T	R	P	S	A	E	R	L	O	I	R
E	G	O	Y	U	K	F	X	U	P	A	P
T	S	I	W	R	M	T	I	D	O	M	H
S	A	D	B	N	A	P	G	I	D	N	O
H	Y	D	R	A	T	L	K	U	E	H	D
K	P	Q	U	D	T	Z	C	I	B	G	O
F	E	G	A	L	A	X	Y	V	N	I	N
C	A	S	T	L	E	G	I	A	P	J	U

PUMPKIN   CRUMPET
IGGY   SAUROPOD
CASTLE   GALAXY
ASTEROID   HYDRA
MATTA   TARXIG
TAIL   DIMORPHODON

Reading across, down and
diagonally, see if you can find
all the listed words in the
grid above...

ASTRO PUZZLE TIME

MAMMMA WORDS

Professor Hydra has managed to use his evil mangling machine on words. Can you split up the below into sentences?

Astrosaursloveadventures

Teggsisthecaptainofthesauropodandarxigg
yandgipsyarehiscrew

Starvaultsareusedbygalacticbankstotrans
portgoldandjewelsbetweenplanets

Nargnettlescanguessifyouaregoingtoeat
themandstingyou

Teggsandhisteammanagedtoimprisonprofes
sorhydraandreturnthemachinestothesafe
handsofdoctorfrankensaur.

Chapter Seven

TUDOR CUD

The Time Shed blazed back into existence in a cold, quiet courtyard. It was the middle of winter and very dark.

"We've arrived," said Professor McMoo, dancing around the shed like his hooves were stuffed with firecrackers. "At last, we've pitched up in the past! I've been dreaming of this for years. Tudor kings! Brave explorers! Unbelievably smelly toilets! All of that, out there waiting!"

"The toilets can *stay* waiting," said Bo, turning up her nose. "Ugh!"

"If a ter-moo-nator comes after me I might need one in a hurry," Pat confessed.

"Go now before we leave," Bo advised.

"Just don't splash the tea bags," called McMoo.

"We'd better stick those ringblender thingies on," said Bo, clipping hers in place. She had "decorated" it with pink and green nail varnish but luckily it still worked.

Pat finished his business and clipped his own ringblender into place. "Let's see what we look like," he said, crossing to a special mirror that Yak had given them. It showed the way they would appear to human eyes.

"Wow," said Bo, eyeing her reflection. She looked just like a Tudor lady! "Look at me — beef in a bodice! I make a pretty funky person, if I do say so myself."

Pat grinned at his handsome human reflection. "From bullock to baron, in the blink of an eye. And, Professor, look at you!"

McMoo smiled. "From a no-bull bull to a noble*man*!" The professor's reflection was lordly as you like. The mirror showed a large, powerful-looking man with curly hair and a huge moustache.

"Well, that's quite enough gawping in the mirror." He pulled on the CHURN-lever and all the fantastic technology vanished back into the walls and floor – if anyone forced their way inside they would see just a wooden building. "Let's see what's outside. Filth! Plague! No potatoes! Oooh, I do love history!"

"I'll love it better when that *ter-moo-nator* is history," said Bo.

"Er, Professor?" asked Pat nervously. "If this is the king's palace, won't people wonder what we're doing here and, um, try to lock us up and kill us and things?"

"Not if they don't see us, Pat," said McMoo with a reassuring smile. "We'll stay out of sight as much as we can."

The three cows left the Time Shed and sneaked into the palace through a nearby gatehouse. They shuffled along gloomy passageways lit by flickering torches. The chill of winter was in the stone, and they shivered as they clopped quietly up some steps towards the sound of chatter and laughter.

"Someone's having fun," Pat whispered.

Sneaking further along the corridor, they glimpsed several women folding sheets in a grand bedroom and gossiping.

"Chambermaids," whispered McMoo. "Let's listen in on their chat."

"What a boring waste of time," Bo complained.

Pat looked at McMoo. "Shouldn't we get on with finding the ter-moo-nator, Professor?"

"A chambermaid's job takes her all over the palace," McMoo reminded them. "They may well have *seen* the ter-moo-nator—"

"– and so they could give us a clue about where to find it." Pat gazed in awe at McMoo. "You're a genius, Professor!"

"True," agreed McMoo. With a wink, he led the two of them closer to the bedroom doorway.

"Just think," a lanky woman said as she plumped up a pillow. "The king's new wife is coming here this very night!"

"I hope she sticks around longer than the last one," said a spotty girl beside her.

"Of course," McMoo whispered. "December 1539 – that means King Henry is getting ready to marry his fourth wife, Anne of Cleves. He ties the knot on 6 January 1540 . . ."

"Oh, Molly, you *are* lucky being her lady-in-waiting," the lanky woman went on. "They say she's as lovely as a summer's day . . ."

"Yeah, a summer's day when it's raining poo-poos!" The voice was gruff, sour – and very familiar. "Pah! Still, better get ready to meet her, I suppose. The king should be greeting her in the main hall any time now . . ."

Bo's jaw dropped. "That sounds like—"

"It can't be," squeaked Pat.

"It is!" McMoo murmured.

A large woman came thumping out of the room and wobbled off down the corridor with a sneer on her face. The cows ducked out of sight as she went past. She looked *exactly* like the dreaded farmer's wife from their own time, Bessie Barmer!

"Clodhopping clover clumps," exclaimed Pat, trembling. "What is *she* doing here?"

Visit **www.stevecolebooks**.co.uk for
fun, games, jokes, to meet the characters
and much, much more!

Welcome to a world where dinosaurs fly
spaceships and cows use a time-machine . . .

Sign up for the free Steve Cole monthly
newsletter to find out what your
favourite author is up to!